# The Pea or the Flea?

S0-DOP-383

Written by
Karen Hoenecke

Illustrated by
Mirielle Levert

Which is longer, the tail or the snail?
the tail

Which is shorter, the flower or the tower?
the flower

Which is heavier, the coat or the boat?
the boat

Which is lighter, the shell or the bell?
the shell

Which is bigger, the tree or the bee?
the tree

Which is smaller, the pea or the flea?
the flea

A flea? Don't jump on me!